# Marvelous Mona

## and her journey to self love

# Marvelous Mona

### and her journey to self love

Written by Grace Motahari
Illustrated by L. Knight

Mona went to school one day,
A happy, smiling girl.

But when she went outside to play,
Her classmates changed her world...

Mona loved the monkey bars
And hanging upside-down,

But then the boys came up to her
And said things that made her frown.

Why does your belly poke out like that? It looks so round and chubby.
Your arms have hair all dark and black. They look so coarse and stubby!

Mona jumped off the monkey bars
And put her jacket on.

Even though it was
hot outside
It felt like the sun
was gone.

Her dad had hair on his big, strong arms
And grandma had a soft belly.

They ate rice for dinner all the time
Instead of peanut butter and jelly.

Mona never thought that
How she looked was strange or weird

Until the boys came up to her
And filled her thoughts with fear.

After school she went back home
And cried on mommy's lap.

Mommy asked her what was wrong.
Then put on her thinking cap.

Mona, I am just like you
My arms have soft, black hair.
The other girls do have this too,
But the color isn't there

Some people are born with chocolate eyes
Or blue eyes like the sea.
Some people have our dark, black hair
Or hair as yellow as cheese.

Some people have bellies soft and round
And others firm and tight.
So don't let anyone tell you
What body type is right!

We all come from different families
From different parts of the world.

But that's what makes us all unique
My special, little girl!

Like flowers growing in a field
not every one's the same

So love yourself
for who you are
And never be
ashamed!

Mona went to school again
And walked in tall and proud.

She went back to the monkey bars
And there she shouted loud:

What did Mona do
When she was done playing outside?

She helped the other boys and girls
Love themselves instead of hide!

I love your curly, bouncy hair!

Let's try his
curry and her
sticky rice!

Don't be afraid of who you are;
Just take Mona's advice!